The Hugglefish

Adapted by Andrea Posner-Sanchez
from the script "Henry's Hugglefish" by Jennifer Hamburg

Illustrated by Fabio Laguna and James Gallego

 A GOLDEN BOOK • NEW YORK

randomhousekids.com
ISBN 978-0-7364-3360-0 (trade) — ISBN 978-0-7364-3361-7 (ebook)
Printed in the United States of America
10 9 8 7 6 5 4 3 2 1

enry Hugglemonster and Daddo are in Rainbow Falls to do some hugglefishing! This is Henry's first time, so Daddo is showing him what to do.

"First we stomp into the water," says Daddo. "Then we throw out the net and roar three times. *Roar. Roar.* ROAR! And then we lift the net to see all the Hugglefish we've caught!"

Daddo is surprised to see he didn't catch any Hugglefish at all.

As Daddo explains that catching Hugglefish can be tough, Henry yells, "I caught one!"

Henry did it on his first try! Daddo is very proud.

"Aww! He's so tiny and cute. I'm going to call him Little
Levon. Can I keep him, Daddo?" Henry asks.

"Well, Hugglefish are usually happiest out here in
nature, but let's give it a try," Daddo says. He carefully puts
Little Levon in a bag of water.

"Hey, everybody! Come meet my new pet!" Henry cries as he runs into the house. He puts the Hugglefish in a bowl on the kitchen table and introduces Little Levon to his family. Everyone loves him!

Momma and Daddo leave to put baby Ivor down for his hugglenap, and Henry sprinkles some food into Little Levon's bowl. Before long, Henry, Summer, and Cobby hear a strange popping sound.

"Is it me, or did Little Levon just get a little bigger?" Henry asks.

"He's definitely bigger!" says Summer.

"Yup," agrees Cobby.

Then they hear the sound again. *Pop!*

Momma and Daddo come back into the kitchen and see that Little Levon now fills his whole fishbowl!

"Little Levon's not so little anymore," Momma says.

"He's bigger and better!" says Henry. "And he needs a bigger place to live."

Henry and Cobby carry Little Levon upstairs to the bathtub. "Here is your new home," Henry announces.

Little Levon happily leaps into the air and uses his tail to swat a ball to Henry. When he lands in the water, everyone hears *Pop!*

Now the Hugglefish is too big for the bathtub!

"I don't think we can call him *Little* Levon anymore," Summer says.

"Don't worry, Levon," Henry says. "You're my pet, and I'm going to take *roar*-some care of you, no matter how big you get!"

Henry asks Cobby to invent something that can help them move Levon to Ivor's paddling pool in the yard.

Minutes later, Cobby is back. "Presenting my newest invention, the Slider Rider!"

Cobby places the invention on the bathroom floor. It inflates and unrolls—into the hall, down the stairs, out the front door, and all the way to the paddling pool!

Everyone works together to lift Levon onto the Slider Rider. Then the whole family rides along with him! *Whee! Splash!*

Levon is the perfect size for the pool, until . . . *Pop!*

"Oh, no!" cries Henry. He is worried about where to move Levon next. The Hugglemonsters try to think of a place in Roarsville that is big, fun, and has lots of water. At the same time, they all shout, "The Monster Wave Park!"

Before long, they are on their way to the water park.

"Attention, monsters and monsterettes!" Henry announces. "Presenting the newest, coolest, most *roar*-some attraction at Monster Wave Park— Levon the Hugglefish!"

Levon is a little nervous, and so are the monsters in the pool with him. But once everyone sees Levon play ball with Henry, they all join in.

Then Levon grows. Again. He is wedged between the walls of the river-run ride, and a group of monsters is stuck behind him!

"I think it's time to take Levon back to Rainbow Falls," Henry tells Daddo. "I'll miss him a lot, but I know he'll be happy there."

Daddo gives Henry a hug. "I'm proud of you, Henry. You thought about what would make Levon happy, even if it might be hard for you."

Luckily, Captain Hollander, the airship pilot, is nearby. Cobby and Henry attach a Monster Wave Park banner to the bottom of the airship and use it to scoop Levon out of the water.

Henry and Daddo climb on top of Levon, and Captain Hollander flies them all to Rainbow Falls.

"Up, up, and away!" cries Daddo.

"Home, sweet home," says Henry as Levon happily splashes around in the water. "I'm going to miss you, but I don't think you'll ever get too big for this place! I'll be back soon to visit—so we can play more ball!"